~~RVICE

To

C.O.R.G.I
AND THE PURSUIT OF THE PRINCE'S PANTS

ReadZone Books Limited
www.ReadZoneBooks.com

© in this edition 2016 ReadZone Books Limited

This print edition published in cooperation with Fiction Express, who first published this title in weekly instalments as an interactive e-book.

FICTION EXPRESS

Fiction Express
First Floor Office, 2 College Street,
Ludlow, Shropshire SY8 1AN
www.fictionexpress.co.uk

Find out more about Fiction Express on pages 91–92.

Design: Laura Durman & Keith Williams
Cover Image: Hunt Emerson

© in the text 2013 Ian Billings
The moral right of the author has been asserted.

ISBN 978-1-78322-556-9

Printed in Malta by Melita Press.

C.O.R.G.I

AND THE PURSUIT OF THE PRINCE'S PANTS

IAN BILLINGS

What do other readers think?

Here are some comments left on the Fiction Express blog about this book:

"To say they are enjoying C.O.R.G.I. is an understatement and several of my pupils are desperate to show their parents the first chapter!"
Natalie Johnson, Year 5 teacher at Bicton School, Shropshire

"Every chapter gets better."
Katie D, Somerset

"I have enjoyed the book because it's funny and interesting to read. It made me be at the edge of my seat because I wanted to read on to find out what was going to happen next. I think the book is the best book I've ever read so far!!!!"
Portia M, Worcestershire

"We enjoyed reading your story C.O.R.G.I. and the Pursuit of the Prince's Pants *very much. We thought the story was hilarious. It is a really good book to cheer you up when you are down in the dumps."*
Class 5EP, Westacre Middle School, Droitwich

"The Pursuit of the Prince's Pants is really funny."
Grace, Bedford

Contents

Chapter 1

Dogs on a Mission

Time – just after lunch

Place – somewhere over the
Tower of London

Date – a Friday in September

HRH, or Her Royal Highness to her
friends, was sitting aboard the royal
helicopter nibbling at a crustless
cucumber sandwich. She spotted
the Tower of London far below
her. She pictured her Crown Jewels
safely nestled inside and smiled.

Then another thought entered her royal mind.

"Now where are my little rascals?" she asked between munches. Her valet pointed at her butler who pointed at her chamberlain who pointed at her chambermaid who pointed at her gardener who pointed at the back of the helicopter. There, three small corgi dogs, with parachutes strapped to their backs, were forcing open the rear escape hatch.

Seconds later three small dots were falling very quickly out of the clouds over London. With a loud whoosh, the parachutes popped open and the dots slowed down. The parachutes each sported a Union Jack design, and dangling below were the queen's precious pooches.

* * *

Five hours earlier Prince Cedric had been in Buckingham Palace, lying in the biggest bath he'd ever seen. In fact, it was the only bath he'd ever seen. Prince Cedric was the Twenty-Ninth Cedric of Utter Phalia (there had been twenty-eight Cedrics before him, and that's a lot of Cedrics).

Hardly anyone had heard of Prince Cedric the Twenty-Ninth, or of Utter Phalia. It was a very small country. Some world maps didn't even show it and when they did it was usually lost in the fold of the pages. In fact, it was so small it only had a monarch – Cedric – and one other member of the population – Walter Wiggle, Cedric's valet.

It was such an honour to be a guest of the queen in Buckingham Palace.

Prince Cedric lay back in his bath and dreamed of the fabulous dinner he would enjoy the following evening. He even practised bowing, which is not easy to do in a bath. Try it sometime. He held his rubber duck in the air and announced, "Your Majesty this is the most wonderful evening of my life, Your Majesty. I'm so pleased, Your Maj–"

He was interrupted by a loud "Aaaaaaarrrrrrrrrggggggggghhhhhhhhh!" from outside the bathroom.

Cedric sat up with a splash and said, "Who is argh-ing out there?"

Walter Wiggle, his ever-ready servant, came crashing into the bathroom, saw his naked boss and quickly covered his eyes with a loofah.

"Bad news, Your Majesty! Terrible, awful news. The baddest bad news ever. Remember that time you swallowed a sock?"

"Yes?"

"Well, this is worse than that!!"

"Heavens! Whatever has occurred, Walter?"

Walter took a deep breath and finally said, "It's the Ceremonial Pants of Utter Phalia, sir… they have been…" Then he gulped the longest, most worry-filled gulp ever and finally said, "…stolen!"

"Arrrrrrrggggggghhhhhhhhhhh!" Prince Cedric splashed from the bath, covering himself with his duck. "I can't possibly dine with the Queen of the Engerland place without my Ceremonial Pants. What shall we do? What shall we do?"

The Ceremonial Pants of Utter Phalia had been worn by every Cedric in the country's history and were worth a fortune. They were a large, golden one-size-fits-all pair of pants trimmed in purple velvet and sparkling with rubies and emeralds.

The pants were so heavy they needed a pair of golden braces to keep them up. And they were always worn on the outside of the trousers, of course – otherwise no one would see them!

The pants were also fantastically valuable. Imagine the most expensive thing you can imagine then double it – that's how valuable they were. Of course, to a naughty, bad-deed-doing pant-collector they were absolutely priceless....

* * *

Meanwhile, three floors above the panicked prince, on the very roof of Buckingham Palace, sat a kennel. But this was no ordinary kennel. This was the headquarters of the Canine Organization for the Resolution of Grave Injustices, better known as C.O.R.G.I. The greatest, most secret crime-fighting outfit in the world.

The C.O.R.G.I. kennel was bursting with every hi-tech, top of the range gadget and gizmo needed to catch a baddie. Infrared doggie goggles, radio-controlled bones, self-destructing flea collars and radar guided pooper-scoopers. The lot.

The queen's corgis, known in the Royal Household by their code names – Chester, Holly and Willow – were playing ball outside. Their ears pricked up at the sound of the first scream, and they dashed inside to find out what was going on.

First came 'Chester' – real name James Bone – handsome, rugged and a bit stupid. Very wet nose.

Just behind him was 'Holly' – real name Alesha Vixen – highly trained, highly intelligent, highly glamorous. Great nose for trouble.

The two set to work checking security cameras to locate the source of the scream. Eventually, in lumbered 'Willow' – AKA Horace Crumple – probably the oldest dog ever to fetch a stick.

"I've found it!" Alesha cried.

"Great – what's the action? A kidnapping? A plot to take over the government? Someone threatening to blow up the world?"

"Um… it seems to be a naked man and… some stolen pants…."

"Oh, great!" James growled.

"Don't be sarcastic, young one," said Horace, in his wise old voice, "Remember – from little poodles, Great Danes grow… or was it puppies from Great…? Anyway, I remember during the first jubilee and… zzzzzz."

As Horace's sleepy head landed on his desk with a thwack, an alarm boomed out from Alesha's screen. Horace yelped and just-about-managed not to fall off his chair.

"I've intercepted a video message sent to Prince Cedric," Alesha announced, and then added, "You know – the naked guy."

"Oh right, well I suppose we ought to watch it then," muttered James. "You never know, it might be a ransom demand for his pants!"

Alesha opened up the message:

"Hello, Prince Cedric, it is I, Foo Foo la Diva – the maddest, baddest poodle on Earth. I am your worst nightmare. I have got my paws on the Ceremonial Pants of Utter Phalia and if you want them back – and I'm sure you do – I want paying. 200,000 of your Briterlish pounds and I want it all by midnight on Saturday! Tee hee ho hee ho! BOL*"

Alesha and James exchanged a worried look.

* BOL = Bark Out Loud

"Foo Foo la Diva – she sounds mad!" said Alesha.

"Mad?" replied James, softly, "She's barking!"

"She looks pretty crazy, too," added Horace. "With that pointed nose and blonde wig… she's not like any poodle I've ever seen. You know, many years ago, I courted the most beautiful poodle…."

"OK, OK Horace – let's stick to the mission shall we?" Alesha soothed.

"Well, in that case, you might like to take note of the bright golden flag fluttering behind Foo Foo's head…."

"By Bonzo, Horace is right!" cried James in amazement. "Your nose is still sharp old boy."

"Don't you call me old…." Horace barked, but he raised a proud eyebrow.

"I bet you two whippersnappers don't even know what that means. It means she's at the–"

"The Tower of London," Alesha interrupted. "That's where the pants must be."

"That's right Alesha," Horace replied.

"And," Alesha continued, "HRH will be flying over the Tower this very afternoon… on her way to open that new supermarket in Margate, remember?"

"We've got to be on that helicopter," said James.

Chapter 2

To the Tower!

So it was that the three parachuting pooches were to be found, gently descending towards the rooftops of London. James barked, beckoned to the others and pointed a paw. There, fluttering its finest flutter on the very top of the highest tower of the Tower of London was a bright golden flag.

The corgis landed on the roof of the Tower of London with a grunt, a bark and a yelp. Springing into action, they wrapped up their parachutes, forced open the skylight and dropped down into the room below.

"Spread out!" hissed Alesha.

Horace lay flat on the floor, spreading himself as wide as he could.

"No!" Alesha barked. "I mean go and find Foo Foo!"

For the next few minutes C.O.R.G.I. rummaged and raked, delved and dug, examined and explored every nook and cranny, corner and cupboard of the Tower of London. Finally they came to the Grand Walloping Room – the only room yet to be investigated. James pawed open the door, scurried in and yelled, "Nobody move! I've got a doggie chew and I'm not afraid to use it!"

And nobody moved because there was nobody there to move. Nobody at all.

But there was a large, locked wooden crate. It towered above the short-legged agents and they sniffed around it quizzically. Horace rubbed against it saying, "Ooh, here's a nice rough bit!"

"Stop rubbing yourself against the evidence!" ordered Alesha.

Horace mumbled something to himself and padded around to the back of the crate.

James lifted himself onto his hind legs and read out a notice. Written in crayon and stapled to the crate, it said:

Prince's Priceless Pants Inside.
Whatever you do, do not open.
Please.

James and Alesha gave each other a paws-up. Alesha leapt onto James's shoulders and pulled out her lock picker (cleverly disguised as a squeaky toy). She jiggled the tool inside the lock.

Meanwhile around the back of the crate Horace found another, more official-looking, label. He peered at it, wishing he'd remembered his reading glasses.

"There's a label here, too!" he barked to the others. "It says R…E…G…"

"Quiet Horace, I'm concentrating!" Alesha called out.

Squinting at the notice, Horace continued, muttering to himself, "R…E…G…E…N…T'…S"

"Whatever!" shouted James, straining under Alesha's weight.

"P…A…R…K   Z…O," continued Horace.

"Not now Horace," growled Alesha.

"Wait a minute!" barked Horace, "Listen, it says, 'From Regent's Park Zoo. Danger. Open with c–"

"What?" Alesha yelped as the lock pinged open in her hand.

* * *

Too late, the door sprung open with a deafening creak, to reveal….

Chapter 3

Biting Bedlam!

"Flea!" barked James, suddenly.

"No," said Alesha. "We have to stay here and solve the… argghhhhhh!! Flea, flea, flea, flea!"

10,000 fighting, biting, nipping, skipping, fleas had leaped, jumped, bounced and zipped out of the crate, jaws gnashing. Suddenly the room was swarming with a busy, buzzing band of boisterous bugs. They were looking for some dogs to bite, and they soon found some….

"Flee!" yelped Alesha.

Horace poked his head around the crate, "I thought we had to stay and solve the… arrrrrgggghhhhh!!"

Within seconds all three corgis were scratching away at their bodies in an attempt to evict the hundreds of hungry fleas who had taken a fancy to them.

"Ouch!" shouted James

"Eeeek!" bellowed Alesha

"Tickly!!" giggled Horace.

The fleas flitted and flirted and nibbled and nipped. Between scratches Alesha managed to say the word, "Water!"

And between itches James managed to reply, "I'd prefer a lemonade!"

"We need to get into some water and get rid of the fleas!"

And with that Alesha ran for the door, followed by a trail of eager insects and her fellow corgis. They galloped as fast as their stumpy little legs could take them. Unfortunately, they couldn't see where they were going through the fog of fleas.

Bash! Alesha sent a fifth-century Chinese Twing vase toppling.

Crash! Went a seventeenth-century clucking stool.

Smash! Went the oil painting of Princess Maureen.

On and on, upstairs and downstairs charged the corgis, desperate to rid themselves of the furious fleas.

Of course, it wasn't long before the trail of chaos attracted the authorities. And the "authorities" in this case were two short, well-rounded and rather doddery fellows called Ollie and Ernie. They were beefeaters. At the moment, though, they were ham eaters, as they'd just finished their lunch, and were nibbling a royal mint.

"What's that?" said Ollie, jumping to his gartered feet.

"I think it's a bit of mustard!" replied Ernie, wiping his friend's chin with his uniform sleeve.

"Not this! That!" He yelled, pushing up his glasses and pointing to where the commotion was coming from.

They exchanged a look that changed from curiosity to concern to terror in about two seconds!

"What is it???!" yelled Ernie.

"I don't know!" replied Ollie, clutching his friend, "But it's coming this…!"

And Ollie would have finished the sentence with the word "way", but instead he was suddenly toppled by the three corgis scurrying and scuttling around the corner.

Bing! Bong! Clatter! Shatter! The two beefeaters ended up in a small, groaning heap on the ground.

But the corgis had no time to stop and apologise. They pelted headlong for the open door ahead and the welcoming sight of the Tower of London pond (built 1571) – and with a yelp of joy and bark of relief all three corgis hurled themselves into the green and grimy water. Kersplash! They could almost feel the fleas pinging and ponging off their bodies.

"Phewww!" said James

"Gosshhh!" said Alesha.

"Tickly!" giggled Horace.

From the grand door of the Tower of London two dishevelled beefeaters, their hats askew, peered down at the dogs. With a haughty sniff, they said, "And stay out!"

The doors clonged loudly shut.

James punched the water, splashing his face.

"We've got to get back inside and find those pants!"

Just then, there came an announcement over the loudspeaker, "You pathetic pooches," it cackled. "Call yourselves crime fighters. You couldn't fight your way out of a paper bag."

"It's Foo Foo," gasped Alesha.

"You calamitous canines," the voice went on. "You should have looked down, not up! Tee hee ho hee ho! BOL."

* * *

Whilst all the mayhem at the Tower of London was unfurling, two figures were fretting back and forth in their rooms at Buckingham Palace. One was Prince Cedric and the other wasn't.

"Wiggle!" bellowed Prince Cedric to his bowing servant, "Have I ever told you how stupid you are?"

"Many, many times, sir! Why just this…"

"Well, clearly it's not enough! You have lost the Ceremonial Pants of Utter Phalia and–!"

Wiggle had bowed thirty-seven times in the last minute and was just about to embark on his thirty-eighth when he said, "But they were stolen, your cuddliness!"

"Don't interrupt me whilst I'm interrupting you. I am the monarch. I do the interrupting. Also – you forgot to clean my teeth this morning, you buttered my toast on the wrong side and you've not blown my nose yet! And what were you doing in my PRIVATE dressing room just now? I thought I heard you talking to yourself."

Walter flushed. "Nothing, your high and mightiness," He replied guiltily, drawing a manky hanky from his pocket and taking a step towards his boss.

"Too, too late. I've wiped it myself now!" muttered Cedric, looking down at his moist sleeve. "You are the utter failure of Utter Phalia!"

Now Walter Wiggle had been battered and bruised by his boss's words for many years. "*One more word!*" he thought, "*Just one more word and I'm out of here!*"

"And look – you've forgotten to clip my nails, again!" Prince Cedric wiggled his unclipped fingers before Wiggle's eyes, "I'm wiggling, Wiggle! Wiggle, Wiggle, Wiggle, Wiggle, Wiggle…."

"Just one more word!" hissed Walter under his breath.

Cedric paused, leaned forward and pulled his most patronizing face which he'd been practising in the mirror for the last ten minutes and said verrrrrryyy slowly, "Wigggggg-llllleeeeee!"

"That's the word!" Walter exploded and started the rantiest rant he'd ever ranted, "I work my fingers to the bone for you, I cook, I clean, I polish, I tweak, I plump, I strain. I'm at your beck and call 25/8 and this is how you repay me!" And with those words (which he had been practising in the mirror for the last ten years), Walter reached for his battered hat and placed it on his head. Only it wasn't his battered hat at all – it was something white and hairy but it seemed to fit him perfectly.

Before his boss registered entirely what had happened (he was still chanting, "Wiggle!"), Walter stuffed the item up his coat, leaving only a few fair hairs peeking out. He looked about, located his hat, clonked it on his head and flounced out.

Prince Cedric was left chanting "Wiggle, wiggle, wiggle, wiggle…" Slowly what he had seen dawned on him, "Wiggle, wiggle… wig?"

Chapter 4

Dungeon Danger

Back at the Tower of London three, very short, four-legged beefeaters were growling to each other under their dog-breath. Not far from the Tower of London pond (built 1571) was a photo booth where fee-paying tourists could dress as beefeaters and have their picture taken. The corgis had soon snaffled three child-size uniforms, donned them and were now making their way back to the Tower. But getting back in was not going to be as simple as that.

"Foo Foo said 'down, not up'," said James. "I wonder what she meant?"

"Don't you see, you chump?" replied Alesha. "She meant down, down to the dungeon underneath the Tower. That's where we have to look next. But how do we get back in again?"

Just as they were starting to hatch a plan they heard a familiar voice, and the voice belonged to beefeater Ollie.

"Who goes there?" Ollie suddenly barked, making all three corgis leap to attention, balancing on their hind legs and saluting with their paws. Horace was about to spill the beans when a second voice, coming from the other side of the corridor and the mouth of Ernie, shouted, "The keys!"

Three pairs of doggy ears pricked up at the word, "keys!"

"Whose keys?" replied Ollie in a militaristic manner.

"The Queen's keys!"

"The Queen's Keys that unlock every room, cupboard and cubby hole in the Tower of London?"

"The same!"

"The Queen's Keys that must not fall into the hands of Her Majesty's enemies or bad-deed-doers upon penalty of death!"

"The same!"

"Hand forth the keys!"

And with a well-polished stomp Ernie marched forward and handed over the keys to his fellow beefeater. Then he twizzled on his well-polished boots, squeaking as he did, and started marching away.

"*I must remind Ollie to have a shave,*" Ernie thought "*His facial hair is getting out of hand!*" Then he noticed something tugging at his sleeve.

"Ern! Ern!" It was Ollie, and he was trotting behind Ernie and hissing at him, "Ern!"

"Not now, Ollie, I'm doing the marching away bit!"

"But you didn't give me the keys. You have to give me the keys!"

"I did give you the keys and I have to say, Ollie, your nails need cutting."

Ollie grabbed at Ernie's sleeve drawing him to a frustrating halt.

"I'm mid-march. You can't stop me mid-march!"

He turned to see a pair of empty hands in front of his face.

"I ain't got the keys, Ernie!"

Ernie was almost nose to nose with Ollie as they both said, "Then … who … has?"

They slowly turned to see the Grand Door of the Tower of London slam shut with a deafening clong and then they heard the sound of keys grinding in the lock.

* * *

On the other side of the door James, Alesha and Horace haired down the slippery, slimy stairs to the dungeons. They soon slowed to a trot as they saw what a strange place they had entered.

In the dank, darkness the corgis could make out instruments of torture, cruelty and mild irritation. The flickering candlelight cast great shadows up the walls and smoke curled and swirled about them. In the distance they heard the plip-plip-plop of dripping water.

"I don't like it here," whispered James. He shuffled to the left, "This isn't much better either."

"Why are we whispering?" whispered Horace.

"Because we don't want to disturb the ghost!" whispered Alesha.

"The goat?" replied Horace, who had bad hearing and worse thinking.

"The *ghost*!"

"There's a ghost of a goat?" asked Horace, "Does it creep up behind you and go…" and he bleated a loud and frightening bleat, which echoed through the dungeons.

"Shhhhh!!" hissed Alesha. And the 'shhhh' echoed down through the dungeons, too.

James decided to take control of the situation, "Listen, pack, let's pull ourselves together. We've shaken off the beefeaters, we've escaped a wild herd of dog fleas. What could be worse than that?"

And, just at that very moment....

Chapter 5

Down in the Dumpster

Creeeeeeeaaaaaaakkkkkk!!!

Suddenly three sets of corgi paws were scrambling and scratching and three sets of corgi mouths were screaming and shrieking in the air. Within a few seconds (which is a little bit longer in doggie years) the three pooches were plummeting, snout first, into a gaping black chasm. A trapdoor had opened beneath them.

Biff, boff, crash, smash!

In a barking muddle, the corgis

tumbled head over tail. Wherever would they end up? Would they survive? Had they nibbled their last doggie biscuit?

* * *

Meanwhile, back at the Palace, Prince Cedric was not happy.

"I'm not happy!" he declared (see, I told you), and stabbed a finger in the air to make his point. But no one was there to witness his dramatic pointing. With sad eyes, he gazed around the empty room.

He'd woken that morning and had to run his own (cold) bath.

"Me, Prince Cedric!" he didn't point his finger this time.

He'd had to brush his own teeth, butter his own (burnt) toast. He'd even had to make his own little eggie soldiers, and they'd come out all different sizes, which he hated.

"Oh dear, oh dear, oh diddley dear!" Diddley was the worst word he could think of. Monarchs don't tend to hear many rude words.

"Oh, flipping heck!" (Apart from these.)

Cedric wandered about his palatial room making sighing noises and swinging his royal arms. He was wondering what he should do.

"Whatever shall I do?" he said (see I told you).

Then something happened to Prince Cedric that had not happened to him for a very long time. He had an idea. This may seem an odd thing to say, but in general monarchs have someone to do that for them. In many countries whole teams of smarty-pants line up to invent ideas for their royalty.

"Open a supermarket!"

"Create a new type of medal!"

"Invent a new sausage!"

"How about an award for hiccupping!"

Are just some of the examples clever people have offered their kings and queens. But this monarch had had only one advisor and that was Walter Wiggle, and not so very long ago he'd flounced out the door vowing never to return.

So Prince Cedric was forced to have his very own idea and this was it:

"I shall find Wiggle and command him to return!"

It wasn't a very good idea, but it was Cedric's very own.

* * *

Meanwhile back at the tunnel, the tumbling continued....

"Woooooowwwwwwwwwwww!"

"Arrgghhhhh!"

"Ouuuccchhhhh!"

...until the three pooches shot out of the end of the chute and into the back of a rather smelly truck.

Clunk, clonk, donk!

* * *

Prince Cedric the 29th of Utter Phalia pranced up and down corridors shouting, "Wiggle? Wiggle? Where's my Wiggle?"

He passed a couple of chambermaids who both realized they were staring at a prince, hastily curtsied and returned to the cutlery they were laying out.

Prince Cedric opened a few cupboards and shouted, "Has anyone seen my Wiggle?"

It wasn't long before it got around the Palace that Prince Cedric was losing his mind. The chambermaid told the footman who told the valet who told the chamberlain who told the head butler who finally told the very queen herself.

By this time, Cedric had become more and more desperate. He was standing on the royal banqueting table in the Grand Hall screaming at the top of his regal lungs, "I want my Wiggle!"

He heard a discreet cough and looked down to see the face of Her Majesty gazing back up at him. She was flanked either side by about twenty confused-looking guardsmen.

"May I help you, Prince Cedric?"

Prince Cedric dropped to his knees, narrowly missing a kipper, and said, "I've lost my Wiggle!"

"You fool!" cried a familiar voice from high above them. "You utter fool."

Cedric looked up…and gasped.

Chapter 6

The Wrath of Wiggle

Stan and Eric were happy binmen.
Nothing delighted them more than to
spend their mornings emptying bins
into the huge truck they drove around
London. They whistled happy tunes
and had a happy skip in their walk. But
this particular morning the whistling
and skipping stopped abruptly as a loud
clunk was heard from the back of the
truck. This was followed by a clonk
and, not long after, a donk.

"What was that?" inquired Stan.

"It sounded like a clunk, clonk and donk, if I'm not mistaken," replied Eric.

They dashed to the back of the lorry where they saw three dishevelled dog faces staring out from amongst the rubbish.

Horace was cleaning some indescribable slime off his glasses. Alesha was tugging something blue and sticky from her hair and James was adjusting his bow tie and leaning from the lorry. He spied Stan and Eric and barked.

"'Ere what are you mangy mutts doing in my truck?" squawked Stan.

"Yeh, get outta there before you get yourselves squished," continued Eric.

"Mangy mutts?" Alesha cried indignantly, but Horace was tugging on her sleeve. The corgis leapt from the van just as a sickening crashy-crunch rang out behind them as the crusher descended to mash the rubbish.

"That was close," said James. He barked his thanks to the binmen (royal corgis are very polite you know) and led his comrades away.

For a few confused, bemused and bewildered seconds, Stan and Eric tried to assess what had happened.

"Where on earth did those dogs come from?… 'Ow did they get in our truck?… And were they really dressed as beefeaters, Stan?" said Eric quietly.

"Nah, can't have been, Eric." Stan replied, pulling himself together.

And with that they hopped on their lorry and sped away in a cloud of confusion.

* * *

As the garbage van caught up with Horace, James and Alesha, the two binmen averted their eyes and stared at the road ahead. The corgis, however, were busy sniffing a lamp post.

"Are you sure?" James asked Horace. "We've got gadgets and gizmos hidden all over London – are you sure this is the right lamp post?"

"I'm pretty sure what we need right now is right here…" Horace replied, scurrying over to another lamp post, "…or here… or… wait a minute!" He scuttled back and forth between passing legs and sniffed about five lamp posts.

"Oh, diddley dear!"

But Alesha's nose, like the rest of her, was much younger and she soon found what they were sniffing for.

She pulled out her little lock picker and, with a small amount of jiggling, the tiny door at the base of the lamp post sprung open. Inside were three small, doggie sized jetpacks which they soon put on.

"See?" scoffed Horace, "Who looks stupid now?"

"You – you've got your jetpack on upside down! To the Palace!"

And with that Alesha and James zoomed into the air followed a little later by a growling and muttering Horace.

* * *

"You fool!"

The voice echoed around the Grand Hall causing a swathe of regal mutterings.

High above on the highest of high balconies, silhouetted against a huge glass window, stood Walter Wiggle. His hands were on his hips and he stared down at the gathered royals and soldiers with contempt.

"Do you think for one moment I'd come back and work for you?"

Cedric nudged the kipper, looking slightly awkward. He grinned uncomfortably at the Queen, nodded at the soldiers and finally said, "Ermmm...."

"Erm?" shrieked Wiggle, "Is that the best you can do?" and with that he leapt from the balcony, snatched at a nearby chandelier and slid down onto the dining table in front of Cedric.

"He squashed my kipper!" moaned the Queen.

Wiggle drew his angry face up to his ex-boss's face (well, at least as close as he could get to it) and said, "Prepare to meet your doom!" He grabbed something from the table and held it threateningly before Prince Cedric's face.

"That kipper doesn't frighten me!" said Cedric.

Wiggle mumbled something and then hissed at the giggling soldiers. He tossed the kipper away, narrowly missing the queen, and grabbed something else from the table.

"A ladle?" scoffed Cedric, "What damage could you do with a ladle?"

Wiggle spat out his words, "I'm going to scoop you!"

Cedric shrieked like a scolded rat, the soldiers hid behind the royal chairs and the queen sighed, rolled her eyes and said, "Here we go…."

Wiggle sliced the air with the ladle and the wind whistled passed the end of Cedric's nose. Wiggle was serious and Cedric was terrified.

"I don't want to be scooped!"

He grabbed at the nearest thing he could find to defend himself. It was a cheese grater. He held it aloft and yelled, "I fight to the death!"

And so saying they launched into a swash-buckling, teeth-chattering, lip-wobbling duel across the dining table. Plates were smashed, glasses broken, teapots upturned.

"Mind my bacon!" cried the queen.

Suddenly two little silhouetted figures appeared on the highest of high balconies and looked down at the madness below.

"Where on earth is Horace?" Alesha asked in the midst of the mayhem.

"He was right behi–" began James as the window behind him shattered into a plethora of pieces.

Alesha ducked, James dived and Horace… shot right over the edge of the balcony, knocked the ladle from Wiggle's hand and landed in a heap before the queen.

"What is the meaning of this?" the queen screeched as two shabby, smelly, beefeater-costumed creatures dashed to their fallen comrade's side.

Cedric and Walter, who had been shocked into silence, stood staring at the scene before them.

"I believe they're corgis, ma'am," whispered Walter.

"Well they're certainly not *my* corgis!" cried the queen. "Arrest these whiffy Yeoman imposters immediately!" she demanded, pinching her royal nose.

The guards began to advance. Alesha shook Horace's shoulder but the old pooch didn't move.

"Great Danes, he's hurt. What are we going to do?" hissed Alesha.

Chapter 7

A Royal Rumpus

Horace lay happily unconscious at the feet of the queen, hiccupping occasionally, as the guards stepped out from their hiding places and began slowly to advance. Alesha looked from Horace to the queen to the guards and back again.

"What shall we do?" she asked again, turning to James.

"There's only one thing for it," he replied. Flinging Horace over his shoulder, he grabbed a toasting fork from the fireplace and leapt onto the banqueting table. His tiny paw hit a porcelain plate and ber-doinged it through the air. It shattered against a painting.

"Uncle George!" shouted the queen.

"En garde!" barked James, brandishing his weapon.

"Who's for a toasting?" Alesha yelped, jumping up beside her companions.

"Where's my dinner?" Horace muttered, disturbed by the crashing plate.

"Grab that toasting fork," cried the queen. "It was Henry VIII's."

Twenty pairs of military hands and one pair of royal hands, loomed before them.

"Grab it!"

"Get it!"

"Give it here!"

Alesha yelped, James barked and Horace whimpered.

Suddenly there was kicking, screaming and shouting and the mightiest game of fisticuffs ever seen on royal premises ensued. The corgis bared their teeth as they'd never bared them before. They snapped, they snatched, they snarled. The soldiers grabbed, groped and grappled.

"Deploy the earrings!" Horace hissed into Alesha's ear.

Alesha unclenched her teeth from a nearby soldier and bellowed, "What?"

"Take off one of your earrings and throw it!"

"Now?"

"Yes – now!"

And so Alesha unclipped an earring and hurled it at the ground. There was a piff, a puff, a surprisingly loud pop and suddenly the room was engulfed in a plume of dark grey smoke.

"Smoke bomb earrings!" howled Horace, triumphantly. "One of my secret inventions!"

"Not so secret now!" barked James.

"Who said that?" asked Alesha.

No one in the room could any longer see anyone else in the room – and what confusion that caused.

"Help!"

"Eekkk!"

"Whose foot is that?"

"Aargh!"

"Owwww!"

"Ooph!"

"Mind my bacon!"

The voices emerged from the mass of swirling, whirling smoke.

Bam, pow, whap, crunch, smack, biff!

"What's going on?" cried the queen as the smoke began to clear and a busby hat landed on her head at a jaunty angle.

She peered into the greyness. Out of the shadows, a pile of battered bodies came into view. She realized they belonged to her guards.

"Useless," she muttered and stormed out of the room, the busby still wobbling on her head.

Prince Cedric poked his head out from beneath the table, where he had been hiding for the last 10 minutes.

"Wiggle?" he whimpered. But there was no reply. Wiggle, it seemed, had vanished.

Later on, having showered, bathed and enjoyed a doggie shampoo Horace, Alesha and James were back in the hi-tech, tip-top-secret kennel above Buckingham Palace. This was their headquarters, their home, their den.

Alesha clipped on a new pair of earrings as James said, "Where's the remote? Let's check through the surveillance footage!"

"I've no idea," sighed Horace, dropping with a thwump into his doggie basket. Suddenly, the plasma screen burst into life, "Oh, found it!" said Horace, dragging the remote out from under him and tossing it to James.

But James almost missed the catch, he was so engrossed with what was on the screen.

And what was on the screen was this....

Lounging in a big, velvet armchair in his room sat Prince Cedric. On his head was a blonde wig and he was sporting a pretty, pink pout.

Is Cedric Foo Foo? thought James.

"Is Cedric Foo Foo?" he said (see, I told you!)

Horace rolled over and scratched his belly.

"Of course not. Why would Cedric blackmail himself?"

"Maybe it's a double bluff." suggested James.

"What's a double bluff?" asked Alesha.

"It's like a treble bluff but with a bit missing!" explained James.

Horace frowned "But that still–"

"Oh stop whittering old man," snapped James, "We need to interrogate this so-called Prince! Break out the muzzle translator!"

"Not the muzzle translator!" Horace and Alesha yelped in unison.

"Yes," said James, softly, "The muzzle translator!"

Chapter 8

Foo Foo Unveiled?

Minutes later three corgi paws were tap-tap-tapping on the door of Cedric's room. It was soon wrenched open and a flushed face appeared. It belonged to the flushed neck and the slightly less flushed body of Prince Cedric. The wig was gone, but the lipstick was smudged clumsily across his cheek.

"What?" said Cedric to the empty space above the corgis, not seeing the dogs below it. Then he looked down.

"Poochey-woochies?" he said as James barged past his legs, Alesha and Horace scuttling behind.

Once inside the room, they gestured for Cedric to join them. He'd seen some bizarre things since his arrival at the palace so he wasn't surprised to see a corgi offering him a chair.

James lifted an eyebrow, smiled suavely, clipped the muzzle to his face then spoke.

"Miaow, miaow, miaow, miaow?" he said, then looked a little confused.

"Wrong setting!" hissed Alesha.

James pressed a little nob on the side of the muzzle and spoke again.

"Mooooooooooooooooooooooooooooo oooo!"

James rolled his eyes.

Cedric looked at him quizzically.

Alesha reached over and flicked the switch. Suddenly they heard James saying, "For goodness sake, I don't want to speak cat or cow or… wait a minute, it's working!" He gave Alesha a big "paws up" and turned to Cedric.

"Good evening!" he said, arching his eyebrow once more.

Cedric waved weakly and wondered if he was going completely mad.

"I represent C.O.R.G.I., a top secret security organization within Buckingham Palace."

Cedric wondered what to say.

"Oh!" was what he decided.

"We saw the ransom demand from Foo Foo la Diva. And we have reason to suspect you may be the person behind the blackmailing!"

"Why would I blackmail myself?" asked Cedric.

"See!" barked Horace.

"Well…" James raised his other eyebrow and said, "We have surveillance footage of you dressed as Foo Foo…"

"Me!" cried Cedric. "Dressed as a crazy poodle? Never!"

James waved a printed screenshot under his nose. "The wig, the lipstick…"

"Oh, well I suppose there is a likeness," Cedric agreed. "But those things don't belong to me. I just found them. I was missing my Wiggle and I thought it might cheer me up to put them on."

"You just found them?" James asked in a mocking voice.

"Yes," Cedric replied.

"And you… you thought it would be *fun* to just *try them on*?" James continued.

"Yeeeeeeeeees," Cedric replied. "I was missing my Wiggle! In fact, I think the wig might belong to–"

Suddenly there was a crack, a smack, a shout and a secret panel in the wall began to revolve… slowly.

A muffled voice came from behind it.

"Nobody move!" it said, faintly.

"Pardon?" said Cedric.

"Oh come on… get a wiggle on," muttered the voice.

Slowly a vexing vision appeared before them.

"Foo Foo la Diva!" shouted James and Cedric.

"Woofity-woof-woof!" said Horace and Alesha.

And there she stood in all her feminine splendour – the blonde wig, the pink lipstick, the flickering eyelashes.

"Give me my money right now, or the pants get it!"

Foo Foo held out a battered box in one hand, and a flaming lighter in the other.

"My pants!! Noooooooooo," wailed Cedric.

"The pounds, princey!" Foo Foo replied, throwing back her head to laugh. "Tee hee ho hee ho! BOL"

"We need to disarm the poodle and grab the pants!" Alesha hissed to James.

"I know," replied James through gritted teeth. "But how?"

Chapter 9

Palace Pandemonium

Foo Foo la Diva smiled a devilish grin at the massed ensemble and wafted the lighter below the box clenched in her manicured paw.

"One more step and 'woof'!" she cackled, "Tee hee ho hee ho! BOL."

The corgis suddenly scrummed together and started growling at each other.

"What are you planning?" hissed Foo Foo, "I can hear doggie mutters!"

Alesha leapt up with a triumphant yelp and yelled, "Do you like my new collar?"

Prince Cedric made admiring noises.
Foo Foo looked suspicious.

"Once Cedric coughs up my dosh I shall be able to afford thousands of such trinkets! Come on, Ceddie, cough!"

But it was James who coughed and, as he was still wearing the muzzle translator, it came out as a human "Ahem!" and he pointed behind Foo Foo. "What's that behind you?"

Prince Cedric's nose turned to where James was pointing his paw.

"You cannot fool me with the 'what's that behind you' ploy! I am afraid of nothing!" yelped Foo Foo.

"Well, that's exactly what's behind you – nothing!"

"Arggghhhhhhh!!!!! I'm afraid of it!" cried Foo Foo quivering, quaking and quavering behind her lip gloss, "Make it go away!"

With Foo Foo distracted, Alesha unleashed her collar and swizzled and twizzled it around her head. It emitted a piercing ray of pure green laser beam. The beam bounced off the chandelier, the mirror and Prince Cedric's crown. It landed on Foo Foo's face, lighting up the poodle's pointy nose like a traffic light.

"Argggggghhhh!" shrieked Foo Foo as fizzling, sizzling smoke started to rise from under her blonde wig. She snatched it from her head and stamped on it with her stiletto. Suddenly, she realized she had revealed perhaps a little too much.

"Dat's dot fuddy!" she said, holding her glowing nose. Clutching the box to her chest she leapt for the door.

SLAM!! She was gone.

"After her, quickly!" shouted James, and three sets of pooch's paws set off in hot pursuit.

"Call out the guards!" cried Cedric, running after them.

* * *

And so the chase began. When the guards heard that a potty poodle was prowling the palace, they quickly jumped into action.

Immediately they split up. Some went upstairs, some went downstairs, some went onto their iPhones to check their lottery numbers. Foo Foo had to be somewhere, but where was that somewhere?

The Throne Room? No!

The bedrooms? No!

The Royal Wee Room? No!

The Palace was alive with clattering, chattering, chasing and racing. Butlers bustled, chambermaids charged, footmen fell over. Every nook and cranny inside and outside the palace was rummaged, foraged and scoured. But no Foo Foo was found.

*　*　*

Suddenly the corgis stopped.

"Wait," said Alesha. "This is ridiculous. We must put our highly-trained skills to the test!"

She started sniffing the floor and immediately stood alert, her whole body rigid and pointing… at what? James and Horace tip-toed in the direction her nose pointed and there, crumpled on the ground, was a bright pink feather boa – exactly the same as the one Foo Foo had been wearing.

"Follow the scent trail!" ordered Horace.

James was away first. His doggie hooter hooked onto the perfumed pong left in Foo Foo's wake.

The other two followed close behind.

They scurried between the legs of the searching soldiers and finally skidded to a halt near a large green wheelie bin outside the royal kitchen.

That's where the smelly scent trail ended!

James trotted towards the bin and placed his doggie ear against the side of it.

He gestured to Alesha and Horace to jump on top. They did and with one huge effort threw open the lid of the bin…

Clonk!

… and looked inside.

There, nestling amidst some discarded kippers and eggs, was Foo Foo La Diva. She looked up and sniffled, "Oh dear – you found me!"

"Of course we found you – we are C.O.R.G.I., the Canine Organization for the Resolution of Grave Injustices. We'd never let a criminal mastermind like you get away!" Alesha replied, standing tall with her paws on her hips (well, slightly higher actually – corgi legs are very short).

"Look," hissed Horace.

"Not now, Horace, I'm enjoying the moment!" said Alesha.

"No, look at Foo Foo's nose. It's all wonky. And that brown hair… I don't think Foo Foo is a real poodle at all."

Alesha gasped and James leapt up to take a closer look.

"Grab my heels," he commanded and Alesha did so, lowering James into the smelly bin.

He grabbed Foo Foo's nose and ripped it away. And there was the sad, lip-sticked face of…

"Walter Wiggle!" chorused C.O.R.G.I. as the twenty gasping guards tumbled outside, followed by a panting Prince Cedric.

"Tee hee ho hee… oh dear!" Walter whimpered, nibbling nervously on a bit of fish.

"So it was YOU who stole the pants! It was YOU who dressed as Foo Foo! It was YOU who blackmailed Prince Cedric!" snapped James.

"Who?" cried Cedric.

"Wiggle!" cried the corgis and guards.

"My Wiggle stole my pants?" shrieked Cedric.

"Not quite!" said a voice, but the voice didn't come from the bin or from Walter Wiggle. It came from the most important lady in all of Great Britain – the queen. "This man may have dressed as Foo Foo La Diva and blackmailed the Prince, but actually the pant thief was...."

Chapter 10

A Royal Revelation

The queen coughed slightly and giggled behind her white-gloved hand, "The pant thief. It was me!"

The corgis jumped down from the bin.

"Woof?" said Alesha and Horace, in surprise.

"What?" said James through his translator.

"You?" came a muffled voice from inside the bin, but the rest of his sentence was lost as the lid fell back down.

Clonk!

James, Horace and Alesha huddled at Her Majesty's feet.

"Allow one to explain," the queen said, smiling at the guards, pooches and prince before her. "You see, for many years, Phil, my darling hubby has been a pant collector. Oh, he's collected pants from all over the world. He has the underwear of heads of state from Australia, from Greece – even a rather stunning pair of boxer shorts from Malaysia!" she chuckled. "So, when I saw Prince Cedric's wonderful Y-fronts, I simply couldn't resist snaffling them. Had I known how precious they were, I would naturally never have taken such a liberty."

The queen looked around at the puzzled faces before her. Every eyebrow in every face was raised up into every forehead.

"This interesting collection hangs in our Private Royal Pant Room – or as I like to call it, our 'Pantry'," she chortled, "and it has remained our little secret… until now. I fear the time has come for the Royal Pant Room to become public. Would you like to see it?"

Every human and doggie head nodded eagerly.

* * *

The queen led them down a narrow corridor to a small door, which she unlocked and threw open.

Everyone crowded round to look in.

The queen began elbowing her way through the crowd. "Do you mind!"

she exclaimed, "Are you not aware that it is forbidden for commoners to touch one without one's express permission?!"

"Sorry," mumbled the guards, the corgis and Cedric in unison, stepping back and bowing.

Inside the room was a dazzling display of some of the finest pants any of them had ever seen in their lives. Big pants, little pants, square pants, green pants, blue pants, diamond pants, plastic pants, pants with frills, pants with braces, pants with bells on, pants with medals on, pants of all shapes, sizes and widths. All were carefully labelled with the country of origin and a date.

"That's my favourite pair!" the queen said, pointing at the Ceremonial Pants of Utter Phalia framed on the wall. She sighed as she said, "Take down Prince Cedric's pants!"

The nearest guard shuffled uncomfortably over to Prince Cedric and began to wrestle off his trousers.

"Hands off!" cried Cedric.

"No you fool!" cried the queen, "I meant those pants – the ones on the royal wall!"

With a bow of sheer relief, the guard stepped forward, lifted the pants from the wall and showed them to all the admiring faces.

"Now that I have come to the end of my tale, I do hope you will all forgive me!"

"Of course, Your Majesty," cried Cedric. "It was nothing but a simple misunderstanding. I cordially invite you to select a pair of substitute pants from my underwear drawer! I have some there I think you will like almost as much."

"You are kind," smiled the queen. "I shall treat you all to dinner tonight at eight by way of an apology!"

"Thank you," chorused the guards, the prince and James.

"Woof woof!" barked Alesha and Horace.

* * *

That night the twenty very excited guards were helping each other into their finest eveningwear. James, Horace and Alesha were grooming each other and looking forward to a huge bowl of doggie food. The queen was busy arranging all the silver cutlery just as she liked it. And in the Guest Room Prince Cedric the Twenty-Ninth of

Utter Phalia was slipping into his Ceremonial Pants – traditionally worn on the outside of his trousers, of course. Then he stepped out into the corridor and strode down to dinner with Her Majesty the Queen of Great Britain.

"One would like to propose a toast!" Her Majesty announced at dinner and everyone muttered in agreement. She stood and raised her glass, "To Pants!"

Everyone stood and echoed her words, "To Pants!"

They sat as the queen said, "Tuck in! Eat as much as you like – we don't like to throw away waste, you know!"

"Even so, I bet in a house this size the bins must have to be emptied every day!" said Cedric.

"Oh, yes!" said the queen.

"What time do they empty the bins?" asked Cedric, very slowly, as a thought entered his head.

"Oh, about now-ish!" said the queen, tucking into her beef.

Cedric looked at the guards. The guards looked at each other. The corgis looked at each other. The corgis looked at the guards as the guards looked at the corgis and every single brain had the same thought at the same time.

"Wiggle!" shouted the guards.

"Woof-woof!" shouted the corgis and all rushed to the door.

"My Wiggle?" cried Cedric, chasing after them.

The door slammed shut loudly behind them, and the queen looked up at the empty chairs.

"Looks as if one is dining alone again," she said, stabbing a potato, "Oh, pants!"

THE END

FICTION EXPRESS

THE READERS TAKE CONTROL!

Have you ever wanted to change the course of a plot, change a character's destiny, tell an author what to write next?

Well, now you can!

'C.O.R.G.I. and the Pursuit of the Prince's Pants' was originally written for the award-winning interactive e-book website Fiction Express.

Fiction Express e-books are published in gripping weekly episodes. At the end of each episode, readers are given voting options to decide where the plot goes next. They vote online and the winning vote is then conveyed to the author who writes the next episode, in real time, according to the readers' most popular choice.

www.fictionexpress.co.uk

WINNER
Education Resources
Award for Innovation

FICTION EXPRESS

TALK TO THE AUTHORS

The Fiction Express website features a blog where readers can interact with the authors while they are writing. An exciting and unique opportunity!

FANTASTIC TEACHER RESOURCES

Each weekly Fiction Express episode comes with a PDF of teacher resources packed with ideas to extend the text.

"The teaching resources are fab and easily fill a whole week of literacy lessons!"
Rachel Humphries, teacher at Westacre Middle School

FICTI●N EXPRESS

Rise of the Rabbits
by Barry Hutchison

When twins Harvey and Lola are given the school rabbit, Mr Lugs, to look after for the weekend, they're both very excited. That is until the rabbit begins to mutate and decides the time has come for bunnies to rise up and seize control.

It's up to Harvey and Lola to find a way to return Mr Lugs and his friends to normal, before the menaces sweep across the country – and then the world!

ISBN 978-1-78322-540-8

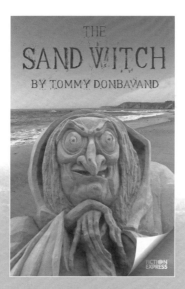

FICTI●N EXPRESS

The Vampire Quest
by Simon Cheshire

James is an ordinary boy, but his best friend Vince is a bit...
odd. For one thing, it turns out that Vince is a vampire. His
parents are vampires, too. And so are the people who live
at No. 38. There are vampires all over the place, it seems,
but there's nothing to worry about. They like humans, and
they'd never, ever do anything...horrible to them. Unless...
the world runs out of Feed-N-Gulp, the magical vegetarian
vampire brew. Which is exactly what's just happened....

ISBN 978-1-78322-553-8

About the Author

Ian Billings was born at a very young age and has done lots of things – some of which we can mention. He is 5' 7" tall in his socks and the same length lying down. Among his hobbies are hiccupping, wobbling jelly and waving at goats.

Author of the popular *Sam Hawkins: Pirate Detective* books (among others), Ian has also written over fifty professional pantomimes and episodes of CBBC's *ChuckleVision*. He has an MA from Birmingham University and is going back next year for the rest of the alphabet.

Ian is one of the only stand-up comics for children in the world and performs globally, including in Qatar, Switzerland, Egypt, Russia, Thailand, Vietnam, Jordan and Australia. He has worked in over 3,000 schools.